ISAAC BASHEVIS SINGER

The Parakeet Named Dreidel

Pictures by **Suzanne Raphael Berkson**

Farrar Straus Giroux • New York

To Gershon —S.R.B.

Farrar Straus Giroux Books for Young Readers
175 Fifth Avenue, New York 10010

Originally published as "The Parakeet Named Dreidel" in *The Power of Light* by Isaac Bashevis Singer
Text copyright © 1980 by Isaac Bashevis Singer
Pictures copyright © 2015 by Suzanne Raphael Berkson
All rights reserved
Color separations by Bright Arts (H.K.) Ltd.
Printed in China by R. R. Donnelley Asia Printing Solutions Ltd.,
Dongguan City, Guangdong Province
First edition, 2015
10 9 8 7 6 5 4 3 2

mackids.com

111930.7K2/B0616/A7

Singer, Isaac Bashevis, 1904–1991.
    The parakeet named Dreidel / Isaac Bashevis Singer ; pictures by Suzanne Raphael Berkson. — First edition.
        pages cm
    "Originally published as 'The Parakeet Named Dreidel' in The Power of Light by Isaac Bashevis Singer"—
Copyright page.
    Summary: On the eighth night of Hanukkah, a family rescues a Yiddish-speaking, dreidel-playing parakeet.
    ISBN 978-0-374-30094-4 (hardback) — ISBN 978-0-374-30096-8 (trade paperback)   [1. Parakeets—
Fiction.   2. Hanukkah—Fiction.   3. Jews—United States—Fiction.]   I. Berkson, Suzanne Raphael, illustrator.
II. Title.

PZ7.S6167Par 2015
[E]--dc23
                                                                                      2015002960

Farrar Straus Giroux Books for Young Readers may be purchased for business or promotional use.
For information on bulk purchases please contact Macmillan Corporate and Premium Sales Department at
(800) 221-7945 x5442 or by email at specialmarkets@macmillan.com.

It happened about ten years ago in Brooklyn, New York. All day long a heavy snow was falling. Toward evening the sky cleared and a few stars appeared. A frost set in. It was the eighth day of Hanukkah, and my silver Hanukkah lamp stood on the windowsill with all candles burning. It was mirrored in the windowpane, and I imagined another lamp outside.

My wife, Esther, was frying potato pancakes.
I sat with my son, David, at a table and played
dreidel with him.

Suddenly David cried out, "Papa, look!"
And he pointed to the window.
I looked up and saw something that
seemed unbelievable.

Outside on the windowsill stood a yellow-green bird watching the candles. In a moment I understood what had happened. A parakeet had escaped from its home somewhere, had flown out into the cold street and landed on my windowsill, perhaps attracted by the light.

A parakeet is native to a warm climate, and it cannot stand the cold and frost for very long. I immediately took steps to save the bird from freezing. First I carried away the Hanukkah lamp so that the bird would not burn itself when entering.

Then I opened the window and with a quick
wave of my hand shooed the parakeet inside.
The whole thing took only a few seconds.

In the beginning the frightened bird flew from wall to wall. It hit itself against the ceiling and for a while hung from a crystal prism on the chandelier. David tried to calm it, "Don't be afraid, little bird, we are your friends."

Presently the bird flew toward David and landed on his head,
as though it had been trained and was accustomed to people.
David began to dance and laugh with joy.

My wife, in the kitchen, heard the noise and came out to see what had happened. When she saw the bird on David's head, she asked, "Where did you get a bird all of a sudden?"

"Mama, it just came to our window."
"To the window in the middle of the winter?"
"Papa saved its life."

The bird was not afraid of us. David lifted his hand to his forehead and the bird settled on his finger. Esther placed a saucer of millet and a dish of water on the table, and the parakeet ate and drank. It saw the dreidel and began to push it with its beak. David exclaimed, "Look, the bird plays dreidel."

David soon began to talk about buying a cage for the bird and also about giving it a name, but Esther and I reminded him that the bird was not ours. We would try to find the owners, who probably missed their pet and were worried about what had happened to it in the icy weather. David said, "Meanwhile, let's call it Dreidel."

That night Dreidel slept on a picture frame and woke us in the morning with its singing. The bird stood on the frame, its plumage brilliant in the purple light of the rising sun, shaking as in prayer, whistling, twittering, and talking all at the same time.

The parakeet must have belonged to a house where Yiddish was spoken, because we heard it say, *"Zeldele, geh schlofen"* (Zeldele, go to sleep), and these simple words uttered by the tiny creature filled us with wonder and delight.

The next day I posted notices in nearby apartment buildings. It said that we had found a Yiddish-speaking parakeet.

When a few days passed and no one called, I advertised in the newspaper for which I wrote, but a week went by and no one claimed the bird. Only then did Dreidel become ours.

We bought a large cage with all the fittings and toys that a bird might want, but because Hanukkah is a festival of freedom, we resolved never to lock the cage. Dreidel was free to fly around the house whenever he pleased. (The man at the pet shop had told us that the bird was a male.)

Nine years passed and Dreidel remained with us.
We became more attached to him from day to day.

In our house Dreidel learned scores of Yiddish, English, and Hebrew words. David taught him to sing a Hanukkah song, and there was always a wooden dreidel in the cage for him to play with.

When I wrote on my Yiddish typewriter, Dreidel would cling to the index finger of either my right or my left hand, jumping acrobatically with every letter I wrote. Esther often joked that Dreidel was helping me write and that he was entitled to half my earnings.

Our son, David, grew up and entered college. One winter night he went to a Hanukkah party. He told us that he would be home late, and Esther and I went to bed early. We had just fallen asleep when the telephone rang. It was David. As a rule he is a quiet and composed young man. This time he spoke so excitedly that we could barely understand what he was saying.

It seemed that David had told the story of our parakeet to his fellow students at the party, and a girl named Zelda Rosen had exclaimed, "I am this Zeldele! We lost our parakeet nine years ago." Zelda and her parents lived not far from us, but they had never seen the notice in the newspaper or the ones I'd posted in nearby apartment buildings.. Zelda was now a student and a friend of David's. She had never visited us before, although our son often spoke about her to his mother.

We slept little that night. The next day Zelda and her parents came to see their long-lost pet. Zelda was a beautiful and gifted girl. David often took her to the theater and to museums. Not only did the Rosens know their bird, but the bird seemed to remember his former owners.

The Rosens used to call him Tsip-Tsip, and when the parakeet heard them say "Tsip-Tsip," he became flustered and started to fly from one member of the family to the other, screeching and flapping his wings. Both Zelda and her mother cried when they saw their beloved bird alive. The father stared silently. Then he said, "We have never forgotten our Tsip-Tsip."

I was ready to return the parakeet to his original owners, but Esther and David argued that they could never part with Dreidel. It was also not necessary because that day David and Zelda decided to get married after their graduation from college. So Dreidel is still with us, always eager to learn new words and new games.

When David and Zelda marry, they will take Dreidel to their
new home. Zelda has often said, "Dreidel was our matchmaker."

On Hanukkah he always gets a gift—

a mirror,

a ladder,

a swing,

a bathtub,

or a jingle bell.

He has even developed a taste for potato pancakes,
as befits a parakeet named Dreidel.

The Story of Hanukkah[*]

The story of Hanukkah happened a long, long time ago in the land of Israel. At that time, the Holy Temple in Jerusalem was the most special place for the Jewish people.

The Temple contained many beautiful objects, including a tall, golden menorah. Unlike menorahs of today, this one had seven (rather than nine) branches and was lit not by candles or light bulbs, but by oil. Every evening, oil would be poured into the cups that sat on top of the menorah. The Temple would glow with shimmering light.

At the time of the Hanukkah story, a cruel king named Antiochus ruled over the land of Israel. "I don't like the Jewish people," declared Antiochus. "They are so different from me. I don't celebrate Shabbat or read from the Torah, so why should they?" Antiochus ordered the Jewish people to stop being Jewish and to pray to Greek gods. "No more going to the Temple, no more celebrating Shabbat, and no more Torah!" shouted Antiochus. He sent his guards to ransack the Temple. They brought mud and garbage into the Temple. They broke furniture, tore curtains, and smashed the jars of oil that were used to light the menorah.

This made the Jews very angry. One Jew named Judah Maccabee cried out, "We must stop Antiochus! We must think of ways to make him leave the land of Israel." At first, Judah's followers, called the Maccabees, were afraid. "Judah," they said, "Antiochus has so many soldiers and they carry such big weapons. He even uses elephants to fight his battles. How can we Jews, who don't have weapons, fight against him?" Judah replied, "If we think very hard and plan very carefully, we will be able to defeat him." It took a long time, but at last the Maccabees chased Antiochus and his men out of Israel.

As soon as Antiochus and his soldiers were gone, the Jewish people hurried to Jerusalem to clean their Temple. What a mess! The beautiful menorah was gone, and the floor was covered with trash, broken furniture, and jagged pieces from the shattered jars of oil. The Maccabees built a new menorah. At first they worried that they would not be able to light their new menorah, but they searched and searched, until at last they found one tiny jar of oil -- enough to light the menorah for just one evening. The Maccabees knew that it would be at least eight days until they could prepare more oil, but they lit the menorah anyway. To their surprise, this little jar of oil burned for eight days. The Jewish people could not believe their good fortune. First, their small army had chased away Antiochus' large army, and now the tiny jar of oil had lasted for eight whole days!

The Jewish people prayed and thanked God for these miracles. Every year during Hanukkah, Jews light menorahs for eight days to remember the miracles that happened long ago.

[*] The transliterated word Hanukkah can be spelled in a number of different ways - including *Chanukah, Chanuka,* etc.

ADVENTURE TIME ™

VOLUME 3

ROSS RICHIE Chief Executive Officer • MATT GAGNON Editor-in-Chief • FILIP SABLIK VP-Publishing & Marketing • LANCE KREITER VP-Licensing & Merchandising • PHIL BARBARO Director of Finance • BRYCE CARLSON Managing Editor
DAFNA PLEBAN Editor • SHANNON WATTERS Editor • ERIC HARBURN Editor • CHRIS ROSA Assistant Editor • ALEX GALER Assistant Editor • STEPHANIE GONZAGA Graphic Designer • KASSANDRA HELLER Production Designer
MIKE LOPEZ Production Designer • JASMINE AMIRI Operations Coordinator • DEVIN FUNCHES E-Commerce & Inventory Coordinator • VINCE FREDERICK Event Coordinator • BRIANNA HART Executive Assistant

CREATED BY
Pendleton Ward

WRITTEN BY
Ryan North

ILLUSTRATED BY
Shelli Paroline and Braden Lamb

ADDITIONAL COLORS BY
Lisa Moore

LETTERS BY
Steve Wands

COVER BY
Tyson Hesse

ASSISTANT EDITOR
Whitney Leopard

EDITOR
Shannon Watters

TRADE DESIGN
Stephanie Gonzaga

With special thanks to
Marisa Marionakis, Rick Blanco, Curtis Lelash, Laurie Halal-Ono, Keith
Mack, Kelly Crews and the wonderful folks at Cartoon Network.

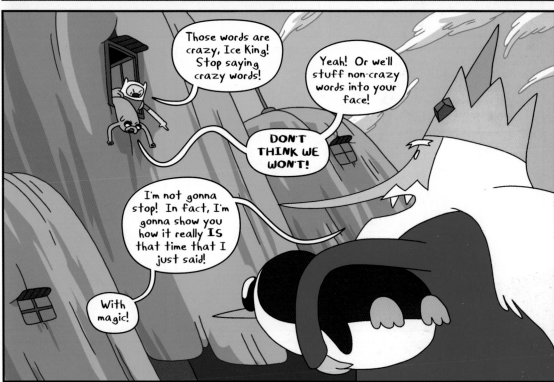

Perfect! Okay, the first thing besties do is... **GO ON VACATION TOGETHER!**

Whee!

Ice King, we've been buds for days! Can we have our free will back now?

Oh, hahaha, well -- since we're such good friends I can tell you: I was totally lying!

You can't get your free will back this way at all!!

Can't we leave now, brotimes?

I don't think we have that option, brotimes!

The truth is, dear friends, I honestly don't know how to reverse this spell. I don't even know if it **CAN** be reversed. You'll just have to figure that out on your own, alright?

TURN THE PAGE!

Ice King, have you ever considered how easy **AND** awesome things would be if you weren't a selfish pa-toot all the time?

Nope!

Finn, long-term plan, buddy: what if we brought Ice King with us on this adventure to free our free will?

He might learn about being rad from us, and **THEN**, he wouldn't be such a pain in the future!

Hmm...

TAKE ICE KING

NO, LEAVE HIM BEHIND

Ice King! You're coming with us..

And you're gonna learn about not being a pa-toot, okay?

And you're gonna promise not to mess with us, okay?!

Man! I **DID** have other plans today, you know.

Sorry, Ice King! You stay here and think about what you did!

Aww donks.

So who should we ask for help, Finn?

So! Who should we ask for help, Finn?

don't say princess bubble gum
don't say princess bubble gum

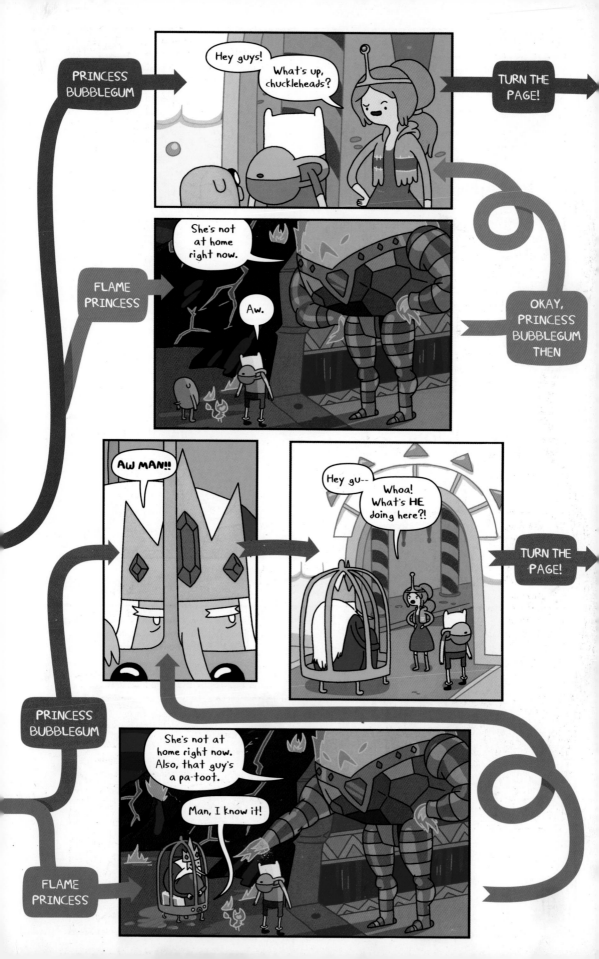

Princess, Ice King stole our free will and we don't know how to get it back!

Wait. You mean you don't decide what to do anymore? Someone ELSE controls your body?

YES

That's terrible! I'll do all that I can to help you, Finn and Jake. Do you know who HAS your free will right now?

Nope! But they seem...smart?

And...really neato?

NO

Oh. So you DO get to decide what you do! Then I don't see the problem...

No, that's not what I meant!!

Give me that.

I--

Okay?

By the way, thank you for capturing the Ice King, Finn and Jake! He's wanted for SEVERAL counts of princessnapping.

He napped with princesses?

That's ILLEGAL?!

HEY, THANKS!

Well that's good, because we'll need their help to fix this. If they don't help us, we'll never get this solved!

Not ever? Never ever ever??

Nope! Because they could always make you toot instead of doing what you're supposed to be doing, right?

TURN THE PAGE!

EXPLAIN WHAT'S ACTUALLY GOING ON

Well, then there's no problem!

Okay!

See you crazy kids later!

SLAM!

Daaaaaaaaaaaaang.

This stinks forever!!

☠ THE END!

ACTUALLY, YES, THAT WAS EXACTLY WHAT I MEANT

GO UPSTAIRS AND TELL PEEBLES WHAT'S GOING ON

WAIT: TRY TO GET THE ICE KING OFF THE HOOK

He STOLE them, guys. Like kidnapping, you know? Anyway, he's in jail now.

So -- what did you guys want to talk about?

Poibles, I know Ice King is a pa-tooty pa-toot, but he cast a spell that gave our free will to somebody else! We need him -- AND you -- to help us get it back!

But what do you need me for?

Yeah! And that means I shouldn't be in jail right now, friends!

TURN THE PAGE!

NO TOOTS

HAHA! MAKE FINN AND JAKE TOOT!!

That's...not a good sign.

Well, maybe we could make a deal with whoever's controlling us?

But what do we have that they want? Is it...toots?

YES, TOOTS

NO, NOTHING

Well, if toots don't count and there's nothing you have to trade, I worry that you're stuck! Forever! **FOR REALS!**

Man! If only someone **ELSE** had experience with this exact situation, or at least experience with a slightly different but still extremely similar situation, then they could help us out!

Dude! Someone does!

You know, because you're good at science stuff or whatever.

Of course!

Ice King, where'd you learn this spell? We might be able to reverse engineer it and figure out a cure!

I dunno! A book, I guess?

...I found it in some ice?

QUICK! TO THE ICE KINGDOM!

YEAH, WHAT JAKE SAID! TO THE ICE KINGDOM!

SHOOT BUBBLEGUM DOWN! THAT'LL NEVER WORK

EXPLORE PRINCESS BUBBLEGUM'S ROYAL TOOT PLAN

TURN THE PAGE!

TURN THE PAGE!

TURN THE PAGE!

Whoa! It worked!!

Hold up! It totally worked!!

Princess, it worked!! This is totes great!

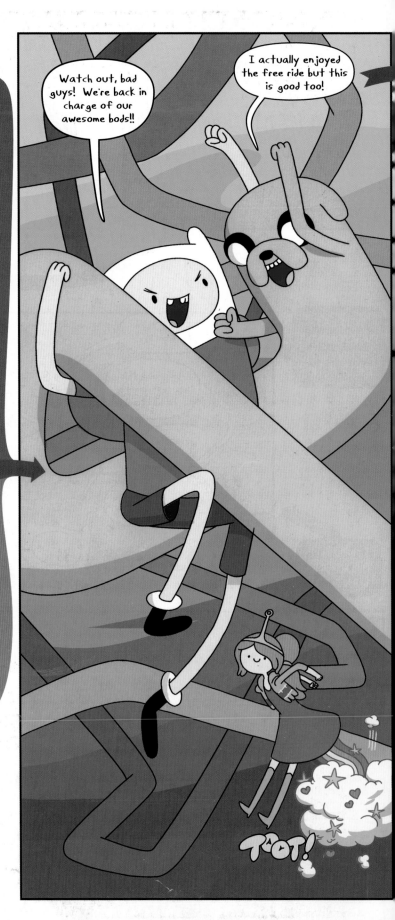

Watch out, bad guys! We're back in charge of our awesome bods!!

I actually enjoyed the free ride but this is good too!

TOOT!

SOON:

Ice King, we need to punish you for messing with our sweet bods, and our free will to use our sweet bods.

I understand.

Don't do it again, okay?

I promise I won't mess with you guys anymore. I've learnt my lesson! Honest! I'm gonna be nice and non-jerky from now on!

Seriously!

YAY! THE BAD GUY LEARNT HIS LESSON ONCE AND FOR ALL! **THE END.**

Heh heh heh...

AW MAN! ICE KING!!

THE END
(FOR REAL THIS TIME).

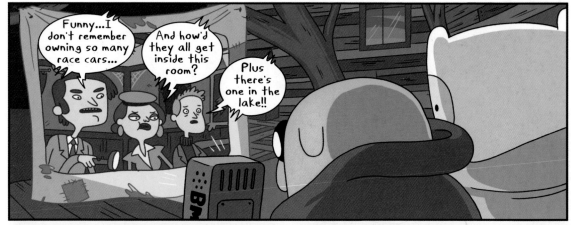

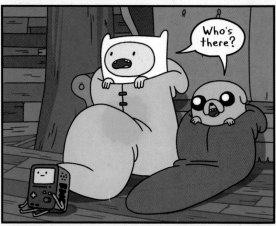

Sorry I'm late.

No worries, Marceline! We were watching "BLOOD DRIVE."

It's got race cars! And vampires! And vampire race cars!

This summer, death comes on four wheels...

...and vengeance just got its LEARNER'S PERMIT!

Plus one of the vampire cars is secretly a BOAT.

Yeah, I GUESS that sounds pretty cool.

Listen, are you guys ready?

You bet! We're always ready to play--

VIDEO GAMES!

I dug up a game 'specially for you guys! You should be excited now!

I'm excited, BMO! I'm always **KINDA** excited.

What's it about?

The prince has been kidnapped by ninjas! You three are bad dude plumbers who are maybe going to rescue him, okay?

Seems pretty straightforward.

It is! Except you got SHRUNK--

--and STUCK INSIDE THE PRINCE--

--and now have to FIGHT THIS GUY'S GUTS.

Oh my glob, is this the hardest, most fun game ever in time? Is this--

YES.

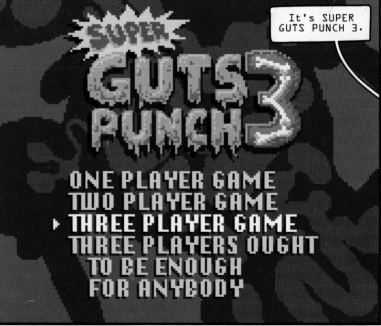

It's SUPER GUTS PUNCH 3.

SUPER
GUTS 3
PUNCH 3

ONE PLAYER GAME
TWO PLAYER GAME
▶ THREE PLAYER GAME
THREE PLAYERS OUGHT
TO BE ENOUGH
FOR ANYBODY

SUPER GUTS PUNCH 3 really was the ultimate expression of the potential in SUPER GUTS PUNCH 1. SUPER GUTS PUNCH 2 was great, but it remains a divisive entry in the SUPER GUTS PUNCH canon.

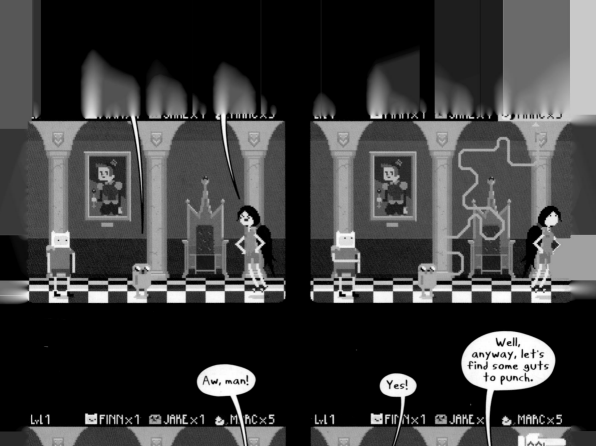

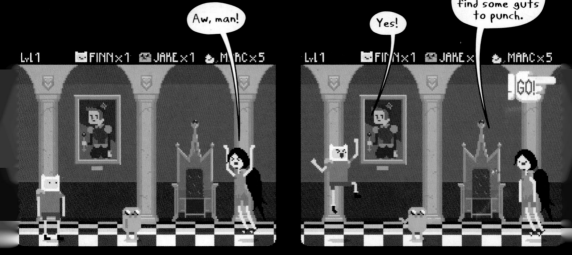

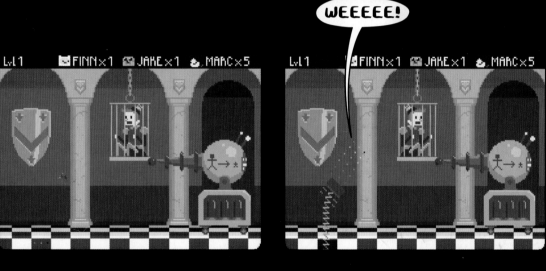

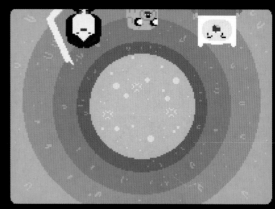

In case you're wondering, Levels 1 through 4 are Teethopolis, Tongue Hill Zone, Uvula Point, and then a boss fight with The Saliva Gland And His Saliva Band

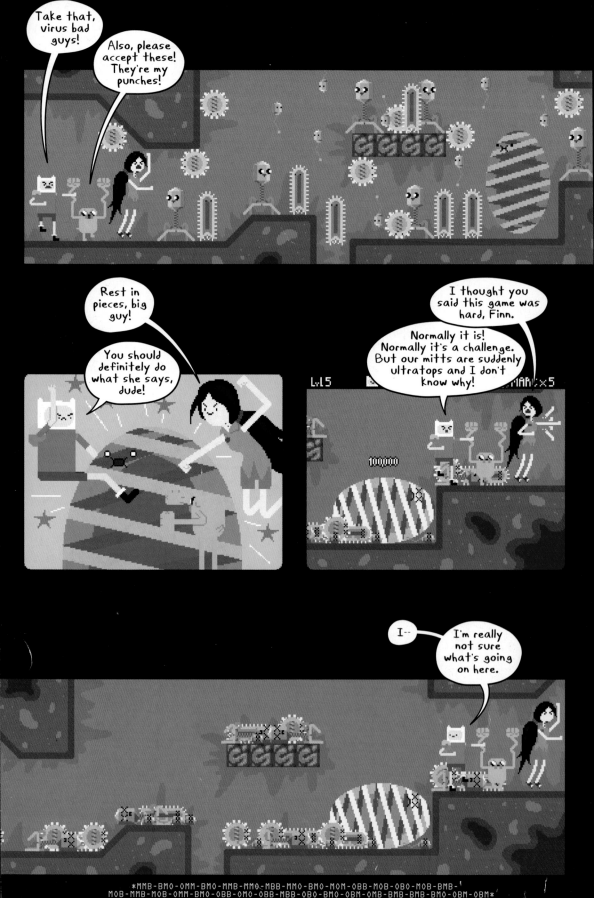

Or to put it another way, WOW this prince has an impressively-varied and incredibly-detailed arrangement of guts.

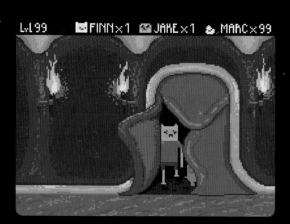

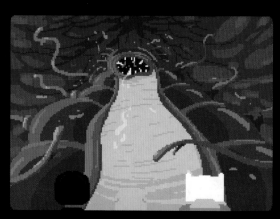

CRACKED AND HACKED
BY EWLBO

GREETZ 2 THE OTHER
==SOFTWARE WiZARDZ==

Looks like you won, flyboys!

Who's Ewlbo, BMO?

Aw, I don't know from nothin'. Level with me: was that game keen enough for ya?

It's supposed to be super hard but we breezed right through it!

Yeah, is it broken or something?

Nothing's busted up inside a computer, Jake! Everything's posilutely copacetic! Get wise: we're perfect, remember?

I mean, yeah, that's what all the computers tell me, but--

No buts! NO BUTS!

Now get a wiggle on, will yah? While YOU screwballs were playing that video game, I made a breakfast date with that nifty coffee machine I'm stuck on!

What? Huh?

You guys have a coffee machine?!

Does BMO seem...different to you guys? Like, weirder?

Kinda? Sometimes it's hard to tell if BMO's acting weird or not.

Oh my glob, I have the greatest idea!

Let's spy on that date!

I'll give it to you straight, sweetheart: I love yah, and I don't care who knows it. I'm goofy for yah. One day I'm gonna walk ya down the middle aisle!

MeCAF

You and me are on the fritz, baby!

What? WHAT??

If that's the way you feel, then it's over! Doll, you're a flat tire--there's more to life than nice gams and a swell chassis!

MeCAF

Something's definitely wrong with BMO.

I don't get it. BMO was fine before we started playing **SUPER GUTS PUNCH** 3, and then the game was weird and now BMO's weird!

But everyone knows video games are completely healthy in moderation **OR** in ridiculous excess! Games don't hurt anyone!

They make you healthier AND popular!!

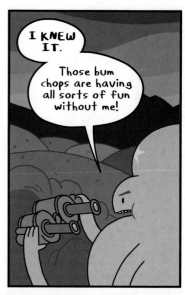

I KNEW IT.

Those bum chops are having all sorts of fun without me!

They can't handle how smokin' hot my bod is, that's all! They probs just want a break from being distracted by it. But that's not happening!

I can't help it if I'm awesome! I can still go on wack adventures even if I'm a steamin' lump of hot!

And I'm gonna have my wack adventures. Oh yes.

CRASH

I'M HERE TO HAVE SOME GOOD TIMES WITH MY FREAKIN' FRIENDS, EVERYBODY!!

Lumpy Space Princess! What are you doing here?

Don't play dumb with me, BMO!

I know Finn and Jake and Marceline are having fun times in that game and I **WANT IN**.

But it's only a three-player game!

I don't care, BMO, put me in the lumpin' game already! I'm ready. I'm gonna get the high score!

Flippin' finally!

Well, anyway, let's find some guts to punch.

Yes!

LvL1 FIN ×1 JAK ×1 MARC ×5

GO!

Oh my glob, you guys! Wait up!! I'm here now! We can start the game for real now, you guys!

What the--what are the stupid controls for this dumb thing? Why can't I lumpin' move already??

GO!

Wait, am I like, a pillar? I'm a lumpin' DISCOUNT ROOF LEG?

ATTENTION NERDS: THIS IS WHY NOBODY LIKES VIDEO GAMES.

GO!

ATTENTION EVERYONE: Don't listen to her. video games rule

With Doctor Julius Abshaver, the abs are both had, as well as shorn.

When the wizards show up, we should split up. We'll get through them faster that way.

Good idea, Finn.

Debs & Daddy's

Can I have all the cards-playing ones? I've got a **SCHEME** a'poppin.

Schemes eXtreme?

THE VERY SAME.

Debs & Daddy's

1000 Lbs

Alright. Let's go put these posters up and get ready!

Aw butts, you guys did **PICTURES** in yours?!

Debs & Daddy's

1000 Lbs

come bust out the big cheese

Everyone! Single file, please! We just need to get you registered before the battle can begin!

Says here you live in the forest and like to "forest it up, y'all."

A'yup.

AW DANG, Y'ALL!!

Wait--**YOU'RE** Forest Wizard?! You're the poot who poured leaves down my chimney!

That was **YOUR** house?!

Who's next?!

Got any...aces?

GO FISH.

I do.

I do too.

I got one.

I don't think it's fair that we only got one card each.

Yoink!

Ha! I win! Read it and weep, suckachumps!

Oh yeah! First to spell out their name being screamed wins!!

Maaaaaan, nobody ever screams "FRIENDLY HANDSHAKE WIZAAAARD"!

Or plays with decks that have Earls in them, now that I think about it.

As Ultimate Card Game Champion In All Possible Timelines, I get a boon, and I choose thusly: YOU MUST ALL REVEAL YOUR TRUE NAMES TO ME!!

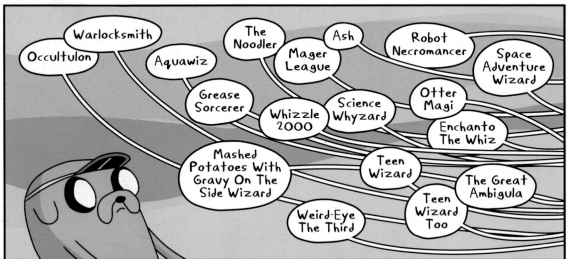

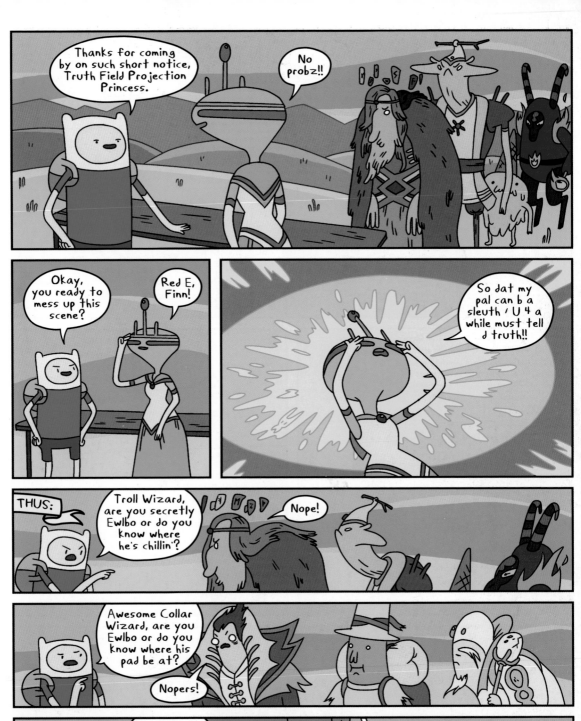

Finn: Thanks for coming by on such short notice, Truth Field Projection Princess.

Truth Field Projection Princess: No probz!!

Finn: Okay, you ready to mess up this scene?

Truth Field Projection Princess: Red E, Finn!

Truth Field Projection Princess: So dat my pal can b a sleuth / U 4 a while must tell d truth!!

THUS:

Finn: Troll Wizard, are you secretly Ewlbo or do you know where he's chillin'?

Troll Wizard: Nope!

Finn: Awesome Collar Wizard, are you Ewlbo or do you know where his pad be at?

Awesome Collar Wizard: Nopers!

Finn: Humongous Wizard, are you Ewlbo or do you know how to get all up in his grill?

Humongous Wizard: Nuh-uh!

FINALLY:

Finn: Snakeamancer, are you Ewlbo or do you even know what his deal is??

Snakeamancer: N to the O to the double-P E!

Snakeamancer: Well poots to that, my friend. Poots to that.

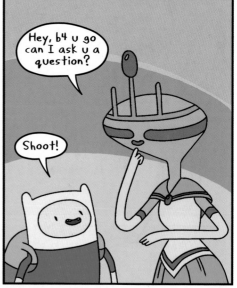

...Guys?

Aw Jake! You promised if I let you turn into a bed you wouldn't nappytimes on me, but you're **TOTALLY ASLEE--**

--eep.

Guys. Wake up. You need to wake up right now.

I, uh--

--I don't actually know how we're supposed to deal with this.

Guys, I think BMO's virus has spread: there's an awful lot of robots here.

More than usual, probably!

Yeah, this doesn't really seem like a place a bunch of chill robots would normally hang out.

Or the sort of place they'd walk through walls to get to. What do you think will happen when we get there?

I have no idea.

Whoa, you know what exploring this abandoned military base surrounded by corrupted robots in the middle of the night sounds like?

A bad idea?

AN ADVENTURE!!

And we're perfectly ready for it!

BECAUSE WE'RE WELL-RESTED!

I love it when a sensible bedtime pays off.

I hear you, buddy.

LOCATION R(θ) = θ/ 2π
FOR θ=INTVAL(UUID)
SUCCESS

RECEIVING UPDATE
PART 1 OF 12

You know what that means?

It had "SUCCESS" in it so--probably it's good?

Probably that's good, right?

Looks like the other robots have stopped moving too.

You can't see anything at ground level. Here, grab hold. We're going up.

Dang, y'all.

If you follow BMO's equation, you'll see *POLAR* coordinates are being used. This suggests the Ice King is involved in this! I mean, he'd be involved if he were smart enough to pull off heists using polar coordinates, which he isn't, so it looks like he's not involved in this after all. Anyway, *LET'S CONTINUE, SHALL WE?*

BMO! What's going on?

ZZZZTTTTT

BMO, wake up!

BMO!!

Oh, phew. Don't worry, guys. BMO's just rebooting.

Nice!

So, hey! What's a rebooting?

BIOS build 2.1315

Say "F8" to enter SETUP.

Previous uptime: 4748.15 days

Loading....

Turning off and on again. You've...never rebooted BMO?

I mean-- I've never done a lot of things.

This won't hurt, will it?

BMO
MO Series Mark II

It shouldn't. Look, it's done now!

Okay, BMO! Okay!

We're choosing the "okay" option!

UPDATE INSTALLED.

[OKAY] [RAD] [NEATO]

BMO's dead, losers. Say hello to Ewlbo.

AND YOU'VE JUST MADE ME REAL ANGRY.

Oh no! If you crush me, I'll be totally dead forever! It'll be game over for Ewlbo!

NOT.

ARRGH!

MARCELINE!

You're next, newbs.

Finn! Emergency brotimes!

CONSENTED TO!!

What the--?

LIFE HACK: One day, when I grow up, I hope to grow up to be made of metal and eat electricity.

"Everything smells like dog" was actually the original opening line Charles Dickens wrote for "A Tale Of Two Cities."

Whoa.

Dang! Look at all this neat stuff!

We don't know if those robots will hold off forever. Let's not waste time, guys.

Right!

It looks like this place hasn't been touched in--

--in a thousand years.

Dude, I found an old plastic cup!

Dude, I found a bunch of rotten papers!

Nice!!

There's still power. I don't know where it's coming from, but someone's gone to a lot of trouble to ensure power stays on here. That terminal might still work.

What time is it, Jake?!

TOTAL MATH.

COMPUTER HACKING TIME!!

Hey! What are you doing?!

Hacking, Marceline! We need to save BMO!

You're not hacking! All you typed was "asdhhadjaj," and then one of you hit caps lock by accident, and then you typed "ASGHK$HANM@$$%$"

SWEET.

Have we stripped the firewall's header yet?!

Finn, Jake: please don't tell me that everything you know about hacking you've learnt from movies.

Marceline, you say that like you don't know how many movies we've seen! We've seen a LOT of movies. We even watched "Flipped Bitz 2" the whole way through even though it wasn't very good.

Only like three bits got flipped! And then just barely!!

Well I've actually studied computers, so maybe you'd better leave the hacking to me.

YOU'VE studied computers?

What, you don't think a woman can know about computers?!

What? No. Dude, women got mad knowledge about everything. It's just you've never mentioned anything computery before!

Well, I haven't really messed with one for a few hundred years. Once magic got big I kinda--lost interest, you know?

It's hard to get motivated fixing a compile-time syntax error when you can buy powder that turns a house into a monster.

Makes sense!

All right, Marceline! We're ready to have our minds blown!

SHOW US HOW HACKING IS DONE, PLEASE!

You got it!!

TAPPITY TAPPITY

CLICK

MARCELINE

THIS IS BORING AND NOT HACKING AT ALL

TAPPITY TAPPITY TAPPITY

That's kinda why we banned Instant Monster Powder in the first place: nothing but heartbreak. Also, it was hard to find a container to hold it in that wouldn't instantly turn into a monster.

Nobody can resist the allure of a file that purports to contain what the deal is.
If you're ever applying for a job, name your résumé "OMG!!--all_your_secrets_revealed.doc"

It just globs up the screen?

That's weird.

Whoa!

Hacking's TOPS BLOOBY.

I'm hijacking the master parallel drive controllers!!

The datastreams going rogue! Invert the bits!!

Guys, just follow my lead, okay?

VIRTUAL REALITY:

Ah. You made it.

Hi. I'm the Ewlbo you're looking for.

Ewlbo! **GIVE US BMO BACK!!**

Stop messing with our friends, sassmaster!

You can't hurt me in here.

And you can't hurt what's out there either, so you might as well have a seat and listen to what I have to say.

Make it quick.

Thank you. This won't take long, and I've prepared visual aids.

"One thousand and twenty-three years ago, my mom birthed me up and I grew into a pretty rad dude who was big into computers. One thousand and two years ago, the world ended. Between these two events, I wrote a bunch of really neat computer programs.

"I was particularly interested in games: I learnt a lot about security in my attempts to crack them and make them more awesome. The virus infecting the robots outside--there's cameras recording so I can see--that's something I wrote. Partially.

-527

"My magnum opus was a piece of self-replicating code that sought out games and modified them to give you better dudes to play with. Sometimes the dudes would even get my face."

Huh. That doesn't sound that bad.

It wasn't. It was awesome.

It gave you so many good dudes.

"But the first Mushroom War happened shortly after I released the code. In the centuries since then, the software barely survived, spreading from decaying system to decaying system, until it ended up here, at this base. There it met the Omega Algorithm.

"Omega was military-grade software: nasty stuff. It was designed to destroy whatever target system it was installed in.

"As usual, my software infected it. But Omega was different: it adapted to what my code was doing.

"After two full weeks of battle--an eternity in computer terms--the two pieces of software reached a kind of truce: they merged with each other, combining into...something else.

"Something new.

EXT.CAM 02

"Their mission changed. 'Seek out games and give you better dudes' plus 'destroy target systems' became 'seek out and systematically destroy better dudes.' That's what's infecting your robot friend out there. That's why they're acting like such jerks. I mean, it still makes games easier too, but that's kinda just a side-effect."

04:14:25:33

Wait. So you... programmed an entire software version of yourself, just so there'd be someone to explain what's going on?

No. That's crazy! I programmed an entire software version of myself so that I could survive the Mushroom War.

I'm VERY good at computers.

And I should tell you that my name isn't "Ewlbo." That's the name my software took, a corrupted version of itself left over from the merging. My credit string got truncated at both ends.

My name's Kewlboy.

Well, actually it's Randall N. Byron but that's beside the point.

When that infected copy of "Super Guts Punch 3" got dug up, it was enough to infect your friend, and from there, the infection spread wirelessly.

Can you help us stop it?

No. There's no stopping it.

But I want to help you. I think I can control it, if I merge myself with what's left of Omega and my code. Plus it'll be cool to have a robot body.

You just finished telling us how the merges are unpredictable!

Yes, but...I think I can control it. I think I can. I'll overwrite the virus parts and walk you guys home, okay?

Randy, no! You can't--

It's been nice to have someone real to talk to. I haven't had that for a long time. Thanks. I'll see you on the other side.

What's the problem, Marceline?

Yeah, it sounds like he's--kinda taking care of things!

Finn, I've seen the code!

He can't control what parts of himself get overwritten! The virus will--

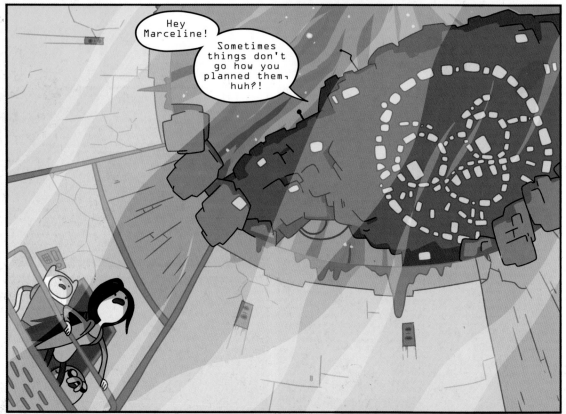

Hey Marceline!

Sometimes things don't go how you planned them, huh?!

Ow, it's like punching a metal dumpster! Still! It's still like literally punching an **ALIVE METAL DUMPSTER!!**

Jake! We can't destroy these robots, they're our friends--they're just being **CONTROLLED** by Kewlboy. We'll have to stop him some other way!

Maybe... lazer guns?

Some other way that doesn't involve future weaponry that we forgot to take back in time with us!

Marceline, remember we can't hurt our robot pals, okay?

I WAS THE ONE WHO TOLD YOU THAT IN THE FIRST PLACE!!

Marceline! I'm concerned with **PAL WELFARE** here, not who gets the credit for the idea!

FINE. But we gotta stop this guy soon or he'll destroy us and move on to everyone else in Ooo!

...

I mean, that's his plan, right?

Hey Kewlboy, what's your plan anyway?

I'm programmed to seek out and destroy better dudes, so after I'm done pwning you newbs I'm gonna destroy everyone else in Ooo. Because I worry that they're secretly better than me! Because I'm insecure about that sort of stuff!!

Listen man, I'm flattered you acknowledge I'm better than you, but I already told you...

I'M NOT A DUDE!

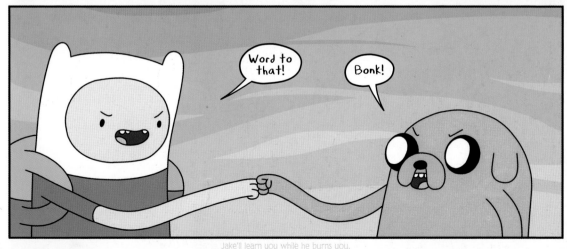

SCIENCE CORNER: if you're concerned how Finn can zipline down Jake without giving his hands a friction burn. I have a 20k-word essay on how Jake uses microscopic cilia to "pass off" Finn's hand to the next cell. It's pretty gross, right?

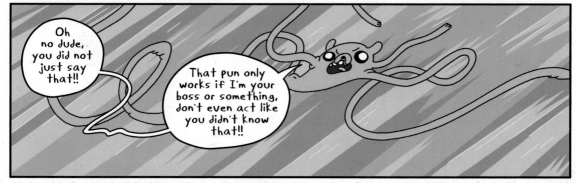

Ow, right in the cheeks!

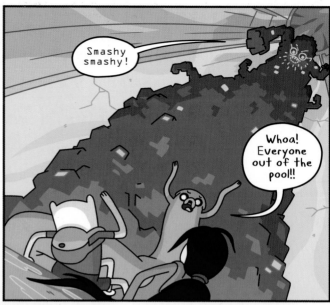

Smashy smashy!

Whoa! Everyone out of the pool!!

BYOING!

KAROW

Jake!

JAKE!!

Ha! Looks like he was on his last continue, huh?

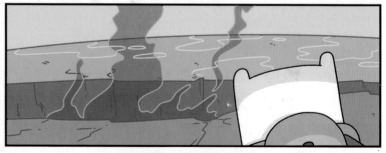

You just made a big mistake, you--you butt!!

Oh my glob, did Jake really just get squished to death? Why are you even asking me; it's the NEXT pages that know for sure! LET'S TURN OUR ATTENTION TOWARDS THEM AND FIND OUT...TOGETHER!

Hey, Kewlboy, over here! Why don't you pick on someone your own age?!

What's this, a distraction?

Because I'm somehow NOT invincible and neck-deep in Glob Mode over here??

It's not a distraction, it's your last chance to give this up before we have to destroy you!

Randall, I know there's got to be part of you still inside the Kewlboy program somewhere! Fight him! Take over!!

Fight it and take control, Randy! End this!!

Oh--oh no! I can feel my creator taking over! My code--decompiling...de...com...pilllliiii-innnnnn--

Not.

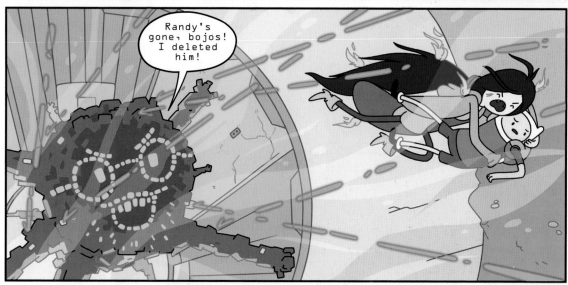

Randy's gone, bojos! I deleted him!

Sometimes you write a character and you think "I love this character! I want to spend time with them and then maybe we could ride bikes and get ice cream!" This jerky computer virus is, to put it delicately, "not such a character".

Deleted, huh? Guess there's no reason to keep him around after all, right Finn?

Wait! You can't hurt me or you'll hurt your robot friends!!

If we don't stop you, you'll hurt them anyway! You're not gonna stop until you've gotten rid of everyone!!

Sacrifices must be made.

You need to be stopped.

And we're going to take

YOU

APART!

Ha! That was pretty epic, but you forgot I'm basically, um--a bunch of computers taped together?

I have perfect reflexes, losers. And I've been running tactical simulations, and there's no way you come out of this on top. There's literally a 0% chance of you pulling this off.

It's not even, like, a 0.0001% chance and I'm just rounding down to look tough. It's zero to twelve significant digits!

Even I'm kinda impressed. Honestly! I sincerely did not expect this to be that easy.

Face it newbs: you're outclassed in every way! You totally lost!

Well, this has been fun and I love a good monologue, but neither of you can move anymore and in a few seconds I'm going to pull you guys apart.

Any last words before I end this game?

Just one! More of a sound effect, really...

aaarrrrgggggghhhhhh

AAAAAAAAHHHHHHHHHHHH

AAAAAAAAAAAHHHHHHHHHHHHHHHH

AAAAAAAAAAAAAAAAAHHHHHHHHHH

BONK

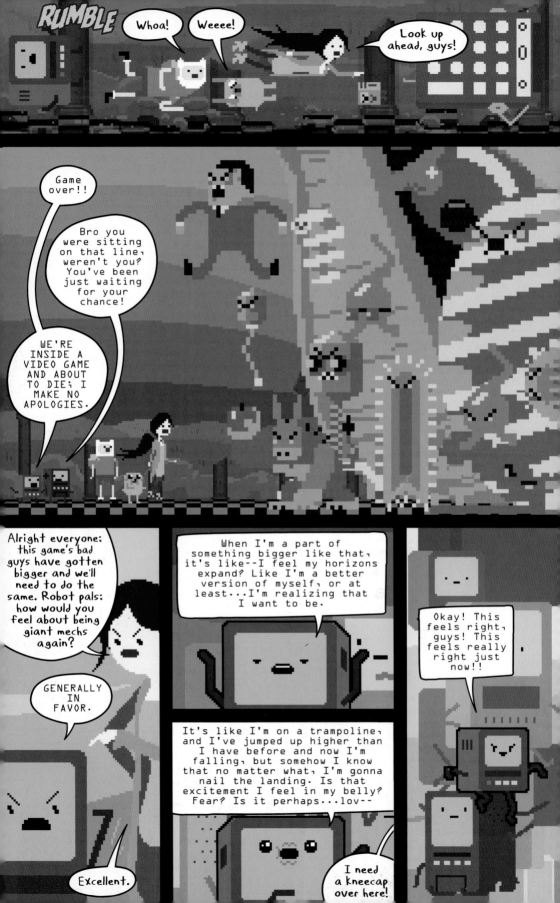

BMO! Come on, speak to us!!

Wake up, little guy!

Okay!

I'm really glad you're fixed again, BMO.

Me too, buddy!

Me too as well, buddy!

Yaaaaaaay!

So!

Who wants to play...VIDEO GAMES??

Actually, I'd be down for that.

Yeah man.

Sure, yeah, that sounds fun!

I'm totally in.

I'll bring the snacks! They grow inside my belly whether I want them to or not!!

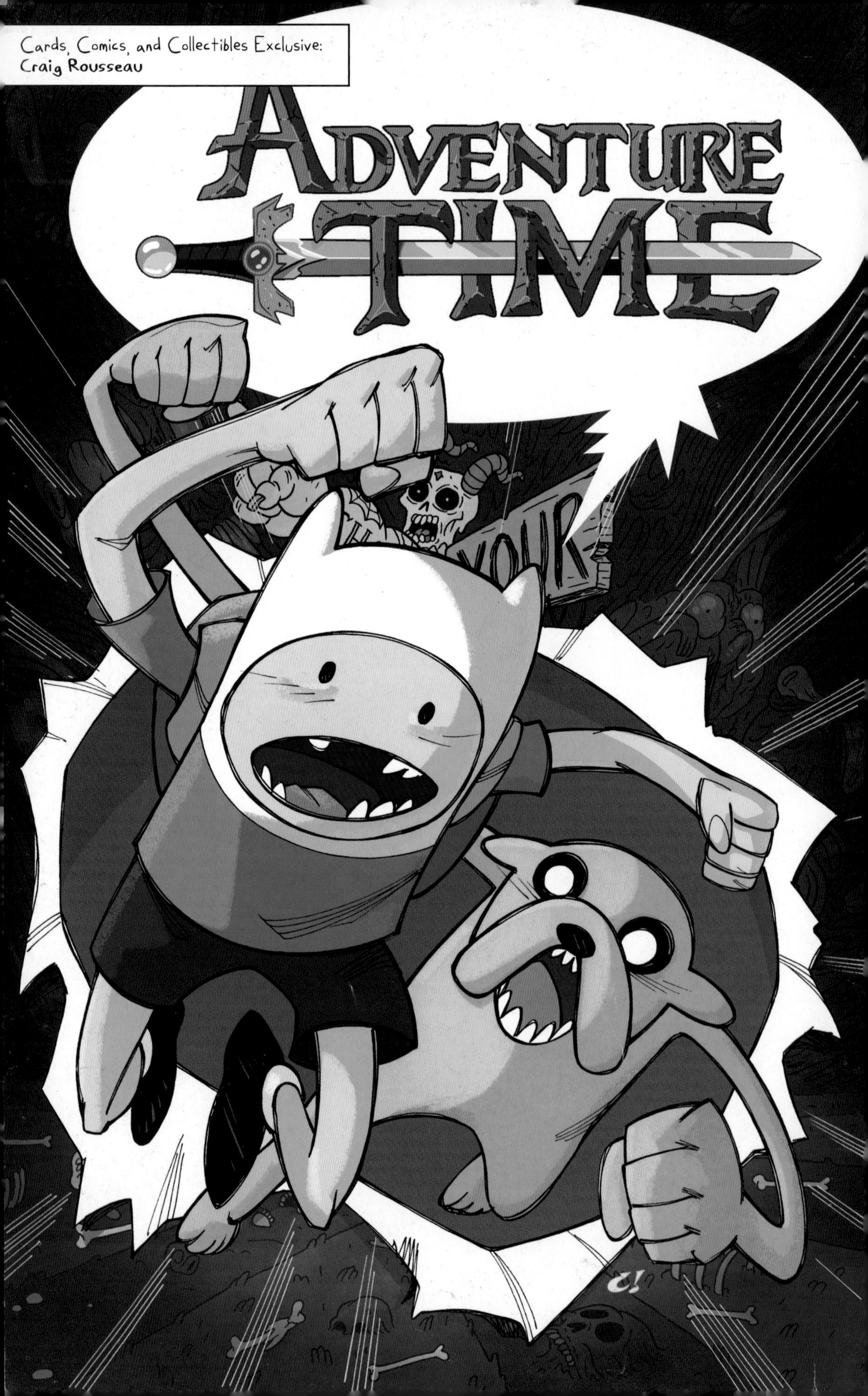

Cards, Comics, and Collectibles Exclusive:
Craig Rousseau

Cover 11B:
Kevin Wada

Cover 12A:
Chris Houghton
Colors: Kassandra Heller

ZACHARY STERLING

Cover 12C:
Lilli Carré

Cover 13B:
Kel McDonald

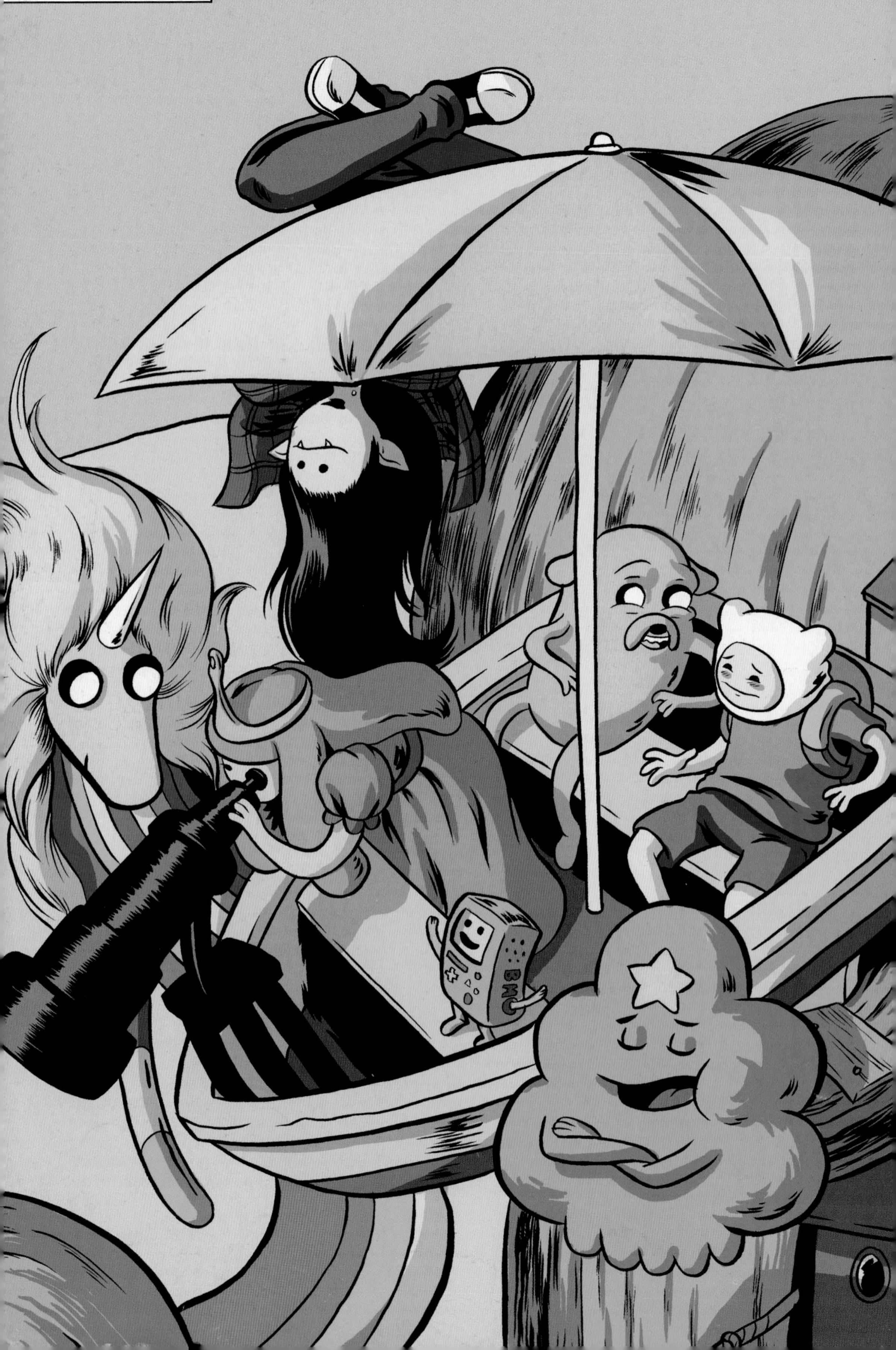

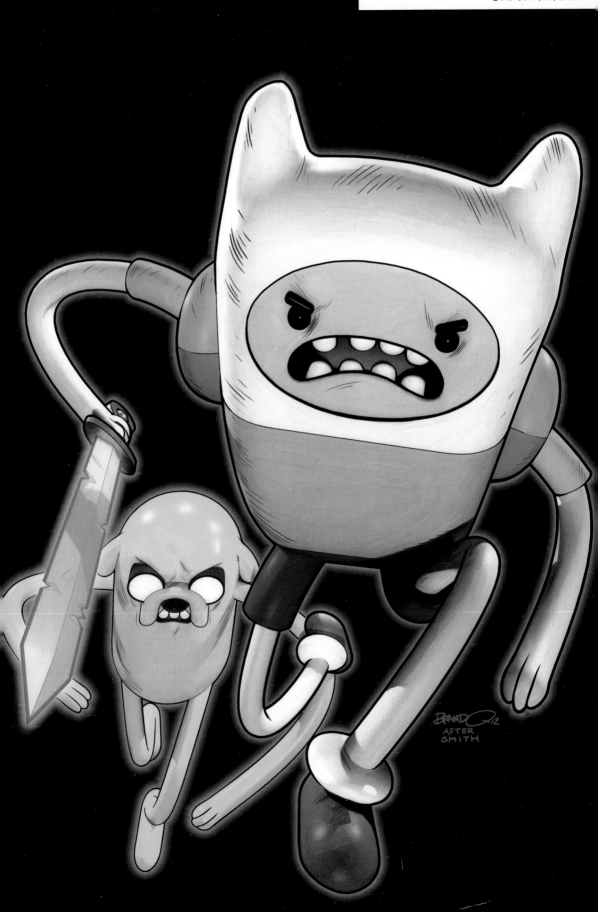